MAKING
THE TEAM

By

Wanda Stutts Jones

PublishAmerica
Baltimore

ISBN: 1-4241-0856-X
PUBLISHED BY PUBLISHAMERICA, LLLP
www.publishamerica.com
Baltimore

Printed in the United States of America

ACKNOWLEDGMENTS

Quote from *The Velveteen Rabbit* by Margery Williams, Doubleday publ., 1922.

For Joe, my inspiration and forever friend.

CHAPTER 1

It's my first day back here in Ridge Point and I haven't talked to any of the kids yet. On my way to eighth-grade reading, an old memory freezes me in slow motion; I stop dead in my tracks. For a full nanosecond I'm transported back in time. And I'm walking through the door of the third-grade classroom with another eight-year-old kid, Jonathan Wheeler. Jonathan was my best friend back then. It was the day after Dad's trial. I feel a cold chill, like the one I got back then, when I remember Jonathan's question. "Is your Dad gonna be on death row?"

It takes a few seconds to come back to the present time. I shrug off the memory, aggravated at my silly self, and open the door, trying to walk in without being noticed.

"Gator!" Jonathan, Dan Fowler and a couple of the guys on West Point Drive shout and I grin back at the old childhood name. I'd been dubbed "Gator" during ball practice. It was a hero name to me. They said the ball stuck to my hands, and my feet held their ground. I'd knocked the ball over the fence, and pitched all winning games. Softball had been my game since I was five, and it had been my first love.

Brittany, the skinny girl next door to Aunt Emma, gives me a toothpaste ad smile. Brittany and I had been good buddies in third grade. Now my feet don't seem to fit under the desk I'm assigned and I can't decide what to do with my hands. Mrs. Cronin gives me a friendly stare and tries to "place" me in her memory. After a minute she forgets me and turns to the assignment on the board.

By the end of the day I've decided it's good to be back. After last period

I end up walking out with Brittany. She smiles so big I can see her gum line. "Your teeth—" I stop. She keeps smiling at me like she doesn't hear. I was about to say something stupid like I thought her teeth sure had straightened out nice.

"So, Scott." She grabs my arm still smiling up at me and I feel a little choked like my chest is constricted and I'm out of air. She wraps my hand around hers and tucks her arm in mine, and I turn stone mute. "Scott, we get together and skate Fridays. You come too. Won't you?" She doesn't wait for an answer "Won't you? Won't you?" She tells me how glad she is to have her old neighbor back. I stammer that I won't be living with Aunt Emma any more. We won't be on that side of town. Now I can ride my bike to school, I say.

Jonathan trots up, gives me a nod and stares at our locked arms. My voice comes back finally. I untangle my arm from Brittany and grin. "As Aunt Emma used to say, Brittany, 'Duty calls.' Mrs. Cronin is expecting some make-up work tomorrow, and I've got to hit the library *and* the books tonight. See you at practice, Jonathan." My voice sounds weirdo, starts out low and ends at a higher pitch.

"Right Dude." Jonathan's voice trails after me, and I turn at the bike stands and wave goodbye. I'm still watching them walk off when Dan Fowler, from Reading class, gives me a thumbs up as he goes by.

"See ya' at practice, Gator?" he shouts. I nod and notice he's come up to Jonathan who pulls out a cell phone, and voice activates it. Brittany turns to beam me another smile and wave. I turn my bike in the opposite direction.

If I could play baseball for the rest of my life, I'd have it made. Sometimes I think of how growing up will be a bum rap. Grown-ups don't play sports, unless it's a few rounds of golf. I play baseball like it's the last game on earth. That's what my first Lakers coach said about me. Our team would win every game with me pitching and batting. I heard him tell my parents that once. "Don't tell Scott," he added. "He'll get the big head so bad, you won't be able to live with him."

Along the highway in front of the baseball field there's a tall thicket of yellow jasmine growing. I turn in through the short gate and park my bike in front of the 10-foot chain-link fence. The baseball dugout is lined-up with guys outfitted for try-outs. They're all yakking and cutting up. I spot Jonathan and give him a thumbs-up. He grins and gives me one back. Coach Gerard calls my name close to the front of the list and a few of the guys yell, "Hey Scotty!" The coach walks over to me. "Heard some good things about you Buddy. Want ta play on the team this year?" He is stout with a gravel voice and no-nonsense beady dark eyes. I just nod and line up to take my turn at bat. I move back a few players and Jonathan and I hang out and talk for a few minutes.

Coach divides us up into Fins and Bucks. "What's a 'fin? "I ask Jonathan.

"I think it's a five-dollar-bill." Jonathan says. "Coach always says weirdo stuff. He's from the east, and he says he used to 'play the ponies.' He means 'horses.' He comes up with some *stuff.*" Jonathan made a track in the red dirt with the cleats on his ball shoe. Now coach motions him over to pitch for the Bucks.

My turn at bat comes up. I hit two high fly balls. and give another one a dead-center 'crack' deep to the outfield. It soars out over the fence, and everybody looks up until it drops in the jasmine vines near the road. Somebody hollers, "Gator is *back*!" Two Fins players cross the home plate and our team celebrates. I feel good all the way to my toes. Like I said, baseball is my game and I'd rather play ball than do anything else in the world.

Another ball is thrown into play just as I come into the third base. Jonathan's pitcher for the Bucks and he gives me a look like he's gonna throw the ball to third. I scoot back onto the base. Dan Fowler's dad and Coach have been standing a little off field talking. Now the coach turns back and eyes the players for a minute. "Who put a new ball into play?" He wants to know. Everybody just stares or looks at the ground for a whole minute. The coach stares right back "Look," he says. "Hear me good. No new ball comes into play before all the players run the bases they're entitled to. You got that, boys?" He looks across at me. "Go on in bud." I trot on in and cross home plate. This time there are no cheers.

During our turn in the field, Jonathan hits a base run and makes it to third on hits from two other Bucks players. He comes in for a run but the batter gets out. I play outfield for our turn and catch a fly ball for two outs. Coach calls time and practice ends.

It's a few hours before it gets dark outside. The guys want me to hang around the field and catch for a while but I tell them I have an errand to run. I have to visit Aunt Emma. When Mom and I were in Huntersburg, Mom and I talked to Aunt Emma on the phone once a week. She's the only family Mom has left, but we haven't seen her more than twice a year in all the time we've been gone. Aunt Em drove very little; and our old car couldn't have stood up to many 200-mile visits, Mom said. Aunt Em and I have always been each other's best buddies. Of course I was little back then; and I was the grandson she'd never had. She'll be as glad to see me, as I will her.

I head back to Main Street, cut through two alleys and turn on West Point Drive. I've never biked down here before or noticed how big the houses are, or how far they are set back from the wide avenue. I ride along the sidewalk and wave at a few people working in their yards.

Turning into Aunt's driveway, I shoot down the short hill and brake near the front door. Racing around to the side—that's how we always went in— I yell for Auntie but she doesn't answer. I walk through the house. I stop near one of my old favorite corners, the window seat tucked in an alcove off the dining room. I used to sit there and gaze at clouds or wait for Mom to come home from her late night job. Aunt and I had read stories there, and once I'd spent the night there with a puppy I'd smuggled in the house. Aunt had quietly come over and covered me up. When I opened one eye she'd winked and smiled her rosy smile. Aunt had taken to calling it the library. Now I buzz on through the house and slide open the glass door to check out the back yard. "Aunt Em!" I shout. And for answer I hear a groan off down the terraced hill. Aunt Em is lying on the ground, and my heart jumps in my throat as I race toward her.

"It's okay, Scott. Help me up," she says.

"Aunt, what happened?" I shout as I stoop over her.

"Oh, reckon I must have tripped over something." She examines her ankle. "Don't think I sprained it," she says. She is still unsteady when I pull her to her feet.

"Boy, you gave me a scare," I say. She leans on my arm and pats my hand.

"School's out, I guess. Your Mom working this evening?"

I nod, as we walk across the flower-bordered patio and go inside. I help her into a chair near one of the wide windows that face the flowerbeds. "Can

10

I make you something to drink? You still drink tea, I bet?"

Her face looks a little haggard, like she's real tired or something. Then she fools me and beams a big smile. "You bet right! Are you buying?"

I grin back. It's like our old routine. "You bet I am!" and I shoot off for the kitchen, snag a large measuring cup from the cabinet and begin to fill it with water. "Four minutes, right?" I shout back as I shove the microwave door closed.

"Three. And slow down, sit down and tell me about school."

I bring back the teapot with tea, cups and a folding TV tray, that I set up between us. "It was good today, Aunt." We look at each other for a long moment. "It's good to be back. I've missed—everything."

I rush back as the microwave beeps.

We talk as Aunt pours tea, and stirs in sugar lumps. "Have you seen Miss Brittany yet?"

"Yeah sure, I saw her. Boy she's pretty now. She's in my homeroom too." I stop and looked at Aunt Em. "What are you asking for?"

"Why Scott, I want to know how things are going. You haven't seen her for a long time and you two were thick childhood buddies." She smiles as she sips her tea. "It means a lot to have a loyal friend, no matter how old you get, Scott."

I get up and trot off to the kitchen to grab a coke for myself. Aunt doesn't drink carbonated drinks but she has a habit of stocking them for my friends and I. "Know what Aunt Em?" I take a long guzzle from the can because I'm about to say something that is embarrassing. "I'm glad I've got you Aunt. As long as you're around I'll never be without a loyal friend."

She stares at me for a moment as if to decide why I'm talking like this. The truth is I don't know myself. "Scott," she speaks slowly and the tired haggard look is back on her face. "Whether I'm around or not, you're my forever friend." In a moment she smiles her merry smile, her tea-stained teeth look stubby in her big round face.

For some stupid reason my face is starting to pucker up like I might cry and I stand up. I stoop down and bury my face in her cool damp hair. "I love you Scott," she says.

I answer in one quick word, "luvyoutoo." I walk over to the glass doors and stand looking out at the backyard. "Say Aunt. I could do some mowing for you every week or whatever."

"That's a fine idea, Scott. And you'll be able to use some extra money."

"I don't mean that you'd pay me, Aunt Em. I mean that I'd do it because I'd like to help you out."

She shakes her head and "tut, tuts" me. "Oh I'd have to pay you. And I know you'd do it for nothing. However-" She stops and changes track. "You may use it to help out at home, you know." I nod.

Aunt Emma never married. She loved a guy way back in the past, and something happened to their love. She once told me she wasn't bitter or even sad. Life goes on, she says. And as for children, she'd had so many as students, and took a personal interest in their lives. Uncle Hugh, her brother, owns her house. But it's been in the family so long everybody just calls it Aunt Em's place. But Aunt has her teacher's pension and retirement so she lives well. She never seemed to need for anything, even when she was helping Mom raise me. Her needs are few and easily met, she says.

"Okay," I say now, and agree that Aunt will pay me for mowing grass once a week and doing chores. "Oh, guess what! I almost forgot to tell you. I'm going out for the ball team. Dad said, 'we'll see,' but I know he was just kidding around. And you know what else? I can use the extra money I earn working for you. I'll need to pay for the uniform and now Mom won't have to pitch in and help me with it."

Aunt Emma rewarded me with her rosy smile and a chuckle of pleasure. "Oh, I am so glad to hear it, Scott. I'll look forward to watching your team play."

"Thanks for everything, Aunt Em," I say and walk over and kiss her on the cheek. She's real quiet as I walk to the door and I turn back. "What?" I ask.

"You're into mind reading, I see." She smiles. "I want to warn you about friends. Remember that an old lady like me has had a number of friends. Be friendly, but don't expect too much of people. Be fair, but don't expect that others will be, at least not often." I study her for a moment, the words not really making any sense. I shrug and walk out the door. My bike is near the front and as I get to the corner of the house I wave. Aunt Emma gives me a merry smile and nods a goodbye.

"I'll call you tomorrow after school," I shout and tear out towards my bike.

That evening I'm lying back on my bed thinking about stuff. Aunt has been like a second Mom to me, and I'm a little worried. I'll find a way to help her, visit her and take care of her. Things have changed, so many things and it's a little scary.

I hear some clanging and rattling in the kitchen and climb off my bed and wade through the clothes and books on my floor. I'm thinking maybe I can head Mom off before she sees my room. There's still homework to do, too. Now, I realize it's too early for Mom to be off work. I go in the kitchen and see Dad is starting supper, It's spaghetti.

He grins and gives me a playful punch on the shoulder. "How's it going fella?" Dad's salt and pepper hair is tied back in a ponytail that ends where most guys' hairline would. It looks cool though; and he says he needs to look cool for a while. I always hate to think of him being in prison like that. It crosses my mind that coming back here might not be so easy for him as he lets on. But we need the cycle shop; it has been a good business for him. That's all he's ever done.

I take out the bread and start cutting it into chunks. I get out the butter and sit down at the table with the baking pan and butter knife. Feeling his eyes on me I look up; then stare at him, puzzled. He swallows hard like he wants to say something; pulls out one of the vinyl-covered kitchen chairs and sits down.

"Scott, I need your help." He looks like he's thinking of getting a tooth pulled.

"Come on Dad." I wave the butter knife. "Cut it out; you're worrying me!"

He wrinkles up his forehead, and I'll swear for a minute that I saw his eyes tear up. "I mean, I need you to work in the shop as my helper." He hurries on quickly. It won't be for long. Just till we get some of the motors rebuilt and a few orders filled." He reaches over and puts a hand on my shoulder. "I promise, son."

"Dad! You know I'll help you. Did you think I wouldn't?" I am even more puzzled. What kind of son does he think I am? It ticks me off.

He sighs, and shakes his head. "It's not your leftover time that I need, Scott. And I'd never ask if your mother didn't have to work so hard." He looks right into my eyes. "I need every spare minute of your time except Sunday when your Mom won't allow us to work."

It takes about ten seconds for me to get it. Then my mouth flops open, but nothing comes out. Finally, I stand up and drop the butter knife on the table.

"But that means—" I stammer and can't say the words.

"Yes, son. It means you won't get to play baseball this spring."

CHAPTER 2

I stand there for a few minutes, wanting to let the words soak down between my ears, but it just doesn't take—not really. One minute the world is my oyster, as Aunt Em used to say. Then in a split-second the whole sorry mess comes crushing down and squashing the best thing in my life. After a long silence I know I'll have to be the first to speak. Dad has turned back to the stove as if to say, "The ball's in your court." Tearing into him like a lion was what I wanted to do. Why did he have to go and spoil everything? First he gets himself thrown into prison. Some sense of reason stopped me. *That* part wasn't fair. He was taken against his will. And he hadn't done anything *wrong,* or at least he hadn't done anything he *knew* was wrong. I smother a groan of misery and know I'd better say something before I do something really stupid like cry.

"Starting when, Dad?" I croak out the words. He hasn't turned around to look at me, and I know he won't.

"Tomorrow, right after school." He says quietly and I leave the room.

* * *

The cycle shop is a big barn of a building that sets back from the street a little further than the auto parts, service station and hardware stores on Main Street. I find the garage door trigger and go inside. In its heyday the cycle shop picked up a lot of business from desert bikers. They roared in from Stockdale, and settled down like a covey of quail until whatever needed fixing got fixed. They tore out again and didn't show-up until time for the next

15

mega biker event in Stockdale or one of the desert towns.

In a way this room looks like its stuck in the past. In one dusty corner hangs a pegboard with shop tools, and an old calendar. I run my finger across the boxes where special biker events are marked for that spring Dad got sent off to prison.

I'm not too anxious to get started on my first helper job. I have three of them. Dad calls them grunt-work. I'm to work on a big cycle he's hoping to sell. I perch on the tall stool at his desk—a long solid wood door he's attached by two chains from the ceiling. It's empty except for a big old-fashioned telephone—no cell phones for us—, a few scribbled notes and a listing of parts needed to repair the cycle. I turn on the stool and stare at the dinks and rusty spots that mar the black paint on the big Harley.

About this time they're lining up at the dugout for practice, I'm thinking. I go to the wall cabinet, drag out a bucket and mix hot water with detergent. Dad said the bike's got to have a thorough washing to make it easier to spot obvious defects. I hadn't bothered to tell coach, or anyone else that I won't be playing baseball. The truth hasn't set in, not all the way, about that. I keep hoping that something will come up and prevent this most important part of my life from being mashed to smithereens. I get out a putty knife and start scraping gook off the cooling fins. Dad says that stuff can make the engine run hot.

The outside door opens, "Hey, how's it going, son?" Dad comes in the door so suddenly that I'm startled out of my daydreaming. I bend over my work like I'm real interested. He takes some paperwork over to the desk and snaps it on the clipboard. . Then he tells me to sit on the big cycle while he checks the rear chain for tight spots.

"How old is this bike anyway, Dad?" I asked the question idly. "I think it's too old for anybody to buy."

Now he straightens up and says, "Give me a hand with this battery."

We set it down by the sink. I make a new batch of detergent and hot water and begin scrubbing it. Dad works from the rear of the bike, tightening every loose bolt or nut he can see. I guess he's decided to ignore my question, thought it was stupid.

Then he says, "It's about the same age as you, Scott." He looks up at me. "And people *do* like old stuff. This will be 'vintage' to the right buyer."

16

I want to say, "yeah, but will you ever get it to run?" But know it's a bad idea. It is time to go home now. Time has passed quicker than I'd expected.

Later, when Mom comes in from work I figure she and Dad have talked about me. She actually walks in my room and doesn't pitch a fit about the "pig pen." Anyway, she comes over and kisses me on the top of the head. She hardly ever does that.

At supper, she says she's home early because Aunt Becky needs her. Aunt Becky is Dad's oldest sister. She got pregnant with her first child late in life, Mom says. Now the baby's due and Mom's all Aunt Becky's got to depend on. Her husband, Frank was killed in a wreck a few months back. Mom is worried and is going to spend the next few days with her. "You know, we've been expecting this, Nick." She tells Dad at supper.

Dad doesn't say anything except, "Sure Lyd, do what you think is best. It's real sweet of you to think of it, honey."

I used to think "Lyd" was the top of a jar, and it took me a while to learn it's short for 'Lydia.' Anyway, Mom isn't promised her job if she's gone more than three days

Dad says it isn't such a swell job working in the grocery store anyway. She's leaving this weekend, she says.

* * *

Later, I decide to go out for a trip around the neighborhood. We live in the North Woods section of town, near the school, and I can go just about anywhere on my bike. I am circling back two blocks up from our house, and this tubby kid waves me down.

"Name's Rudolph Skinner, but call me 'Rudy,' or I'll get all bent outta shape." I shrug, pull my bike over and lean it against a tree. Now he warns me not to get near the begonia bed or he'll catch Ned.

"Who's Ned?" I ask.

He shrugs now and smiles sideways. Ned is another word for 'hell' he thinks; though nobody's ever told him that. He says he's in Reading with me, but I didn't see him this morning. He looks like a brainy kid. Still it's nice to have a boy my own age in the neighborhood.

He asks if I want to catch a few balls. "Don't have a glove," I say.

17

He trots in the house; is back in a minute and pitches a glove at me as we spread out across his front lawn. Says he's outfield on the team when he plays. I tell him I pitch, just like I'm going to be on the team.

"Where were you today?" He asks. "Coach was asking, but nobody seemed to know anything." He throws a wild ball that narrowly misses my knees and lands near the begonia bed. Ignoring his question I retrieve the ball and hold it for a few seconds.

"Aim where you're throwin,' Rudy. Keep control of your throw." He nods and keeps his eye on the ball, reaching high for the catch. His next throw is higher and I have to make a dive towards the tree to catch it. I pay him back with a high ball that he chases down on the other side of the fence. He comes back huffing and panting a little.

"How about something to drink, buddy? He pitches the glove down on the sidewalk.

"Sure." I say, and follow him towards the side of the house. We are about to walk in the garage when he turns and looks at me.

"I know about your Dad, Scott." He says it slow like he's sorry to say it. I stop, rooted to the spot, and just glare at him for a minute. "I'm just trying to be a friend, Buddy," he says.

"Don't call me 'Buddy,' chump!" I holler at him and take off for my bike.

"Scott, I just said what the kids are saying. I mean—"

I turn around and put up my fists. "Who says?" I holler again and feel my face get hot. He takes off his glasses and glares back at me. "Who says?" I demand again.

"It—ah Jonathan told the sixth period class. I mean—he was talking about it in Social Studies. Said you moved away cause your Dad has been up the river for the past four years."

I just sit there on my bike a minute. There's nobody I can rightly be mad at. They're just saying what's true. I want to be mad at somebody, but can't think why I should pick on this guy. My eyes water a little. I grit my teeth and swallow hard. "Rudy," I say; "my Dad was set-up. There was something wrong with some motor parts he'd bought. They said he was receiving stolen property. But he wasn't. He wasn't!" I holler the last part to nobody in particular. I just want to holler at somebody.

Rudy doesn't answer, but just stares at me.

So I just jam my jaws shut and ride on home. I sit in the garage for about five minutes, pretending to mess with a motor Dad's been working on. After a while I shuffle inside and go to bed.

CHAPTER 3

Well, at least I'm too tired to worry about anything. But I've got a twinge of conscience since I got too busy to go by and see Aunt Em. Now I'm thinking that she'll understand how I feel. I can't talk to Dad because it just doesn't seem right to say things like I want to say. I mean how can your tell your Dad that he's ruining your life? Anyway, I guess he knows it. And then Mom would get upset if she thought I was helping out just so she could have things easier. She comes homes lots of time with her feet hurting from standing behind that cash register all day. Truth is, Dad mentioned it to me, or I'd never have thought much about it.

I tell myself that I'll call Aunt Emma tomorrow. She might have hurt herself when she fell. Somehow I feel like there's something wrong. Mom says Aunt Emma and I bonded, like a Mama duck and baby duckling. At the time I'd said, "very funny" and left the room. But there was something to it. I sensed things, kind of like I was into mind reading, as Aunt Em liked to say about me. I fall asleep to the gentle drumming of rain outside my window.

* * *

School the next day turns out easier than I figured it would. I've been hoping people here, especially my friends, will forget the past. I hadn't expected to hide the fact of Dad's being an ex-con, since the whole sorry mess started here in Ridge Point. I only wanted them to know the truth about it. I brought up this point to Dad but he told me to forget it. "Drop it." He'd said without hesitation. "It won't work. Just go on like nothing's changed, and they'll forget about it soon enough." Well, I wouldn't ask Dad what to do about Jonathan's big mouth.

Now I trot outside with a rain slicker, get my bike from the garage and take off. I think about how to tell Jonathan to keep his mouth shut about my Dad. The hard part will be to get to talk to him without losing it, and punching the jerk out. But during the day I'm getting confused. Jonathan gives me a thumbs up and a playful shoulder punch on the playground. And in Reading he'd hollered out at me like I'm his long-lost best friend. I'm beginning to wonder whether Rudy lied. Anyway, I decide not to kick up a fuss during school hours.

As it turns out Rudy sits two seats down from my desk in reading. He gives me a thumbs up and says, "How's it going?" I smile, feeling a little sheepish as I remember all the hollering I did leaving his yard Tuesday evening. He has a stash of sports magazines and we look at them while Mrs. Cronin gossips with some teachers in the hall. I look up and see Brittany. I smile a 'hello', but she doesn't seem to notice; she's staring at me with a puzzled expression on her face. I turn back to the magazine. I keep reading even when Mrs. Cronin comes back and takes attendance.

Some of the kids go to a computer for a reading test and others leave to exchange library books. Rudy leaves too. Mrs. Cronin starts working on something at her desk, but looks up at me once in a while. Brittany and Jonathan leave for library and there's almost no one in the room except a few kids at the computers in the back.

Now, Mrs. Cronin looks over her glasses at me and motions me up to sit down by her desk. She keeps on typing something on her keyboard. She looks young except for a little pot belly and a double chin. She stops and looks at me for a few seconds without speaking. I feel like I'm in kindergarten again; so I don't volunteer any information.

"Scott." She looks down at a paper on her desk for a moment. "This is your third day in school, and I've not gotten grades from your other school, but I believe you're a good student." My eyes find a plastic transparent apple on her desk; and I try to read the mint-wrappings inside the apple. She doesn't seem to notice anything wrong with me not looking at her. I *do* hear the last part about not getting behind on my reading. So I ask to go to the library.

I meet Brittany in the hall and at least she looks at me. We walk over to the water coolers, but just about that time the assistant principal Mr. Thomas decides to come for a drink of water. We stand there for a moment and then Brittany says. "See you at skating Friday night, okay?" I nod okay, and head back down the hall to library.

At lunch I sit with some of the guys from math class. We talk about pre-algebra and how much most of us hate it. Truth was, I'd done okay in it at my old school. Rudy comes up to me and asks if I want to practice Saturday. Coach is pushing the team pretty hard since it's near the end of March and time for season to start, Rudy says. I have to work, I say glumly.

"Well, how about we pitch a few balls after you get off at the shop today?"

"Fine." I say; and I stuff the last half slice of my pizza in my mouth and walk out of the cafeteria. One thing I promised myself this morning was I'd get in Jonathan's face about his blabbing. And I made up my mind to see to it.

After sixth period I wait outside the Social Studies classroom and give him a beckoning nod. "Meet me outside," I say. I walk out to the bike racks and stand, trying to think of something to say that Dad would think is appropriate. Nothing comes in my head.

Jonathan comes out the door, waves off some guys and walks over to me. "What's up Dude?" Somehow Gator, or even Scott would have sounded friendlier. That name, Dude, seemed to put me at a cool distance. Then I remember what Dad had told about taking things calmer. Dad's words came to me "Maybe not Scott. It may not be at all the way you think it is."

Now, we walk over to the faculty car lot and Jonathan leans against one of the vehicles, arms folded, his teeth biting into his lower lip a little. With his chin tucked in and eyes kind of level and indifferent, he looks almost like he used to in third grade. I have to smile. " So, what's goin' on?" He gestures with his head.

I jump right in. " I know you've been saying things about my Dad, Jonathan."

"What things?" He's bites a little more into his lip.

Now I'm getting ticked off. "You know what things! You tell everybody in sixth period that Dad's been sent off up the river. What kind of friend are you, anyway?"

"Maybe I'm not a friend, Bub.

I'm warming to the subject now. "You just keep your yap shut about my Dad, you understand?" I'm shouting now. "Or maybe, you'll be the kind of friend that's an ex-friend with a busted nose." He moves away from the car now, and I can see his ears turn red. They used to do that when he got mad as a kid. " And by the way," I say, "the name's Scott; not Bub or Dude."

I'm feeling pretty shaky now like I know we're about to fight, and I hold my ground and glare as he walks over. "Oh, Scott—ee." He mocks. I'm about to make a dive for Jonathan when we're stopped by this voice of authority.

"Who-oa. Hold it. Hold *it*! What goes on here with you two boys." It's the assistant principal, Mr. Thomas. He retired once and is back filling in. But he's like a permanent fixture. He's known everyone since they were in diapers, and he knows all their secrets. Now he stands here and glares at the two of us from under his shock of white hair.

"You boys are *friends,* for heaven's sake!. What's wrong?" Neither of us says anything; just look at the ground and hope to escape. "Girlfriend, huh? I know. Don't think I don't know what's going on around here. And I know exactly which one it is." His keen blue eyes glare at us a little. "So you're going to give up your friendship. Well, I thought you were smarter than that."

We both shuffle our feet uneasily. I sigh, like I'm tired of running up against brick walls. Nothing's been accomplished. Dad was right.

Mr. Thomas interrupts my thoughts again. "Look boys, what do you say we part friends?"

I look at Jonathan. His expression says exactly what I feel too. I'd rather eat a maggot than shake hands with him. But I stick out my hand anyway. We shake.

At least Mr. Thomas is happy. "That's what I expect from Bristol class guys like you two." He walks over to his car and we watch him as he backs out to leave.

Jonathan mutters under his breath just loud enough for me to hear. "*One* Bristol class guy." He walks off. At least Brittany's not there waiting on him; not that I care one way or the other I tell myself. But I decide he's not off the hook by a long shot. Next time we'll meet in a place where Mr. Thomas won't be around. That's when I'll ring Jonathan Wheeler's bell.

* * *

Most of the bikes are gone and I walk over to mine, feeling pretty disgusted. I can made a bigger mess of just about everything I've come in contact with. All this! And it's less than a week of starting to school in Ridge Point. Guess these problems can't get much worse, unless I go skating with the kids on Friday and bust Jonathan in the chops. This idea makes me feel good.

Before going to work in the cycle shop I run by the house and drop off my stuff. Mom hasn't left yet. "I just feel like I need to be with you during this first week back at school," she said. Truth be known, I agree with her, but don't say so. But what can she do to smooth things out for me. Especially, since I'm not planning to tell her, or Dad, any of the stuff that's going on with me. No one can solve my problems but me.

I'm still thinking about this while working at the shop. It looks like Mom believes I'm suffering from being deprived—not getting to play baseball and all. She doesn't have a clue that anything's wrong between me and the kids. Since I've never had trouble of any kind at school.

That evening Mom comes in my room and checks on me. She thinks I'm handling things well. She means my not getting to play baseball. So I ask her why she's staying to baby-sit me. Before leaving the room she gives me a playful swat. But part of me wants her to stay and call me "poor boy" or something and kiss me on the top of the head. Well, I'll see how she feels about my need for pity after Friday night.

* * *

The Stroller Lanes is a throw back to another time about 20 years ago. It's a portable building that looks like a humungous igloo on the inside with high rafters and an awful sound system. The rink's not far from our cycle shop so I just trot over after work. Vehicles are parked at the curbs, and up and down the block. Some are late evening shoppers. The city is trying to attract more business in the downtown area so some places are staying open until 9:00. Dad says he'll give me a ride home about eleven o'clock.

I rent some old-fashioned skates and whiz over by the snack bar where I order two burgers and fries. In a few minutes some guys from baseball join me and we hang out and talk for a while. Casually, I tell them I'm working in the cycle shop and don't have time for baseball. There's a kind of knot in my stomach when I say it.

Now I look up to see Brittany lounging against the door of the snack bar. She's grinning her possum grin. I stand up wondering if she was first to motion with her finger or if when I saw her I just stood up and opened my mouth like I was trying to catch a fly or something. Either way, I trip over my feet and mumble to my friends "see you guys later," as I skate over to her. She's wearing a golfing t-shirt and skin-tight jeans, all the craze among kids our age.

"Let's skate, best friend." She's grinning that grin and her blue eyes shine like cobalt marbles. I smile down at her—I'm a whole head taller—and grab her arm and we head out across the floor. We skate a whole turn in silence and she notices my feet.

"Scott," She's laughing. "You're wearing those funny skates. Why'dn't you get the roller blades?"

I shrug. "What does it matter? Anyhow-" I stare down at her and we go cannoning into another pair of skaters. They don't know us in the strobe-lighted room, and I shout "sorry," and steer myself and the giggling Brittany back around for another turn. We skate a few more turns around the now crowded floor, managing not to knock down any more skaters. Then we pull in alongside the rail. "Wanna take a coke break?" I ask.

She squeezes my hand for an answer and we skate back to the snack bar. It's almost empty now. "You didn't answer my question." She says.

"Oh, about the skates. Well, tell you the truth, best friend—" I stop and grin at her. "I've never worn roller blades."

She looks like I've told her there's spacemen in Ridge Point. "Impossible." She cups her hand over her mouth to hide some secret glee. "Come on!" She gets up to pull me to my feet. "I'll be the teacher." I do like Brittany an awful lot; but I don't want to try it right now. We sit there and sip our cokes and sort of stare into each other's eyes for a minute while I tear up her wet napkin into neat strips.

"Scott." She sounds like she's going to say something important. I wait expectantly. "You know something? You may be too sensitive about your Dad."

Now I have my eyes riveted on her face.

She leans forward, taking the wet napkin strips from my hands. "I mean it! No one cares about that."

I can't think of anything to say, and we just stare into each other's eyes for another few seconds. Jonathan's big mouth talks up my Dad's history all over the school, but no one *cares!* I don't say anything. And it's just as well since about that time Jonathan breezes up on his blades. He turns sharply at my chair and faces Brittany.

"Scott—ee." He's standing close enough to touch me, and I look up but he just smiles with his teeth together and looks at Brittany. He's got his arms folded again like he's trying to look cool. He asks Brittany to skate and they start to leave. Now he turns and looks at my feet. "Those skates, bro.'" He gives me a thumbs down and grins. "They are *uncool!*"

For a while I sit there thinking again how things have gotten off to such a bad start here in Ridge Point. And I'm wondering if all of it could be my fault as both my parents would most likely believe. Then it crosses my mind how a guy that was my best friend so long ago has turned into such a jerk.

* * *

I'm thinking these same kinds of thoughts again Saturday. I've lost my best friend and he's begun to spread rotten tales about my Dad. We both like Brittany for a girlfriend; and I don't get to play baseball this year. I'm in a self-pity mode this morning. Hard things have happened to me in this little town. I really haven't found out yet that the worst things are still ahead.

* * *

Dad and I work on the big cycle again. He says he knows just the buyer for it. I don't say anything. We replace the old battery cables and I file down the cable terminals until they're clean and shiny. He shows me how to check the front brakes until they have just a half-inch of play. He says we need to flip the tires, and I ask if we can do that next. But he says we'll wait until we get to that part. I do check the spokes, by tapping each one with a wrench and listening for dull clunks that means one is loose. He gives me a spoke-nipple wrench to tighten them with. We work right up to five o'clock.

On the way home I ask Dad to drop me off at Rudy's, and say I'll walk home if he's not back from ball practice. I remember I haven't called Aunt Emma. Then decide there's time to do it later this evening or tomorrow. Swinging off the side of the jeep, I wave Dad on as I spot Rudy.

We pitch a few balls. All the guys were there for practice, he said. Jonathan has been assigned the first pitcher position on the team. Rudy doesn't know if he, himself, will make first team. I don't say anything, but feel kind of sorry for him. He sure tries hard. His catch is improving, but he needs a lot of work on that pitch. I get a good workout chasing all those wild balls and trying to avoid the begonia bed.

I'm taking off across the lawn for one of these retrievals when I look up and see Mom. She's walking up the street. I stop and stare at her for a minute. She had delayed her trip until the weekend; then decided to work today. Saturday's a busy day at the store and she hardly ever gets home before eight or nine o'clock any night. I wave; and stare at her for a minute. She looks worried. Must be Aunt Becky, I think. That doesn't sound right either, so I just stand there and wait for her to walk up to me.

She doesn't say anything, just puts her arm across my shoulders and looks at me /After a long moment she says, "It's Aunt Em."

I feel like a weight's been pressed down on my chest. I pull back and open my mouth but nothing comes out for a minute. Then I manage to croak. "What do you mean, 'it's Aunt Em'?" I'm afraid to look at Mom's face.

"She's had a stroke, son."

"No! I don't believe you!" I fight a terrible pressure behind my eyes and I back away from her.

"I'm so sorry, dear." Her hand squeezes my shoulder. "It's the truth. You'll have to believe it, Scott."

"Oh Mom, I don't want her to die!" I hear myself wail like a small child, and I feel a gut-wrenching pain.

Now I remember Rudy, who's standing in the yard still holding his baseball glove. He doesn't know what to say, and I shake my head as I wave to him before Mom and I trudge over to the sidewalk and walk silently towards our house.

CHAPTER 4

om stayed late at the hospital last night. I know it was immature of me, but I've been expecting the worst. There's a permanent lump in my throat and a general feeling of pending doom. Maybe if I stay away and ignore it, this could turn out just being a bad dream, like a nightmare that you wake-up from in the morning.

It isn't.

The next morning we learn that Aunt Em has some paralysis and probably will be out-of-it. I don't want to think about Auntie. It feels like there's a weight in my chest and I'm too sad to cry. Mom says they're moving Auntie to the Ridgview nursing home.

"That's where old people go to die," I say to Mom. For answer she just hugs me to her like I'm a little boy again. Uncle Hugh shakes his head at me, and turns back to the door. He's come to help Mom with getting Auntie moved. I stare out the window after them long after the car has backed out of our driveway.

Finally I slam out the front door and hop on my bike. Out in the street a bunch of little kids are doing do-nuts and figure eights in their pastel three-wheelers. Further down the street I spot some dads piddling in their garages. A few look like they're dressed for church. I skirt around the little kids, nod and give a half-hearted smile. For a minute I just want to go back home and have a big boo-hoo party for myself. Instead, I just grit my teeth and head on down the street.

I cruise by Rudy's house and he flags me down. "So, how's your Aunt doing, Scott?" Rudy is always a straight shooter.

I just nod my head and say nothing for a minute. "Hey, you going to church or anything?" I ask after a moment. "I mean—what do you say we go out to the baseball field and hit a few balls?"

He studies me like a kind of grim frog; then turns and trots off into the house. He comes back and tosses me the bat, slings a pack on his back and we head down the street to the field. We leave the bikes by the road and climb over the fence. I hit a few fly balls and it looks like I've not lost the magic touch. Rudy makes a few good hits too, but his throwing arm still needs lots of work.

I'm in a better mood; physical activity does that for you; that's what Mom says. I almost forget about Aunt Em, until we look up to see my parents in the jeep. Dad pulls up, turns the jeep onto the grass off the highway and waves for us to hustle. Rudy and I grab our stuff and take off for the gate.

"We want you to come along with us, son" Dad says. "Just leave the wheels and we'll pick it up on the way back. Rudy can you make it back okay on your own?"

Rudy nods. "Sure," he says.

I climb through to the back seat as Dad pulls the jeep on the road "What's up?" I look at Mom.

"Aunt Em," Mom says. "You're all sweaty." I roll my eyes, like what does she expect.

"How'd it go fella?" Dad gives me an easy smile. The early morning sun shows off the silver streaks in his ponytail. I return his smile.

In a few minutes we pull into a parking place near the door of the nursing home and I start to get a knot in my stomach. I give Mom a pleading look that she ignores as she leads the way inside and then down a long hall to Aunt Em's room. I don't want to see Aunt Em in that condition, so I back out and just sort of lurk in the hall by the door. I hate this place. Mom says I need to deal with my feelings about Aunt Em. I just don't want to see her like this. I had told Mom this morning.

"She's dying, Scott."

"No Mama!" The last word was a plea and I had to clamp my jaws shut to fight off tears. Mom tried to touch my shoulder but I shrugged off her hand.

"It's in God's hands, son," she said quietly. Then she kissed the top of my head. Mom had been tough to pull she and I through Dad's prison sentence.

But I wasn't ready for her big idea that we had to face up to losing Aunt Em. Mom was wrong this time. Of course she didn't think so. She would let me grieve and get over it.

"We just can't give up on her," I said. But Mom had walked off.

Now, Dad motions to me and I come in the room, but with what Mom calls my martyr's sigh. Auntie hasn't spoken to anyone since she's been here, so they said. Anyway with the stroke and all, she's not remembering anybody.

I walk to the side of her bed and stare. Her face is paste-white and the auburn hair is dulled with gray. I jump when she opens her eyes and stares back at me. "Scoah—oatt," she rasps the words out. "You're thirteen—now." Her voice sounds tired and the last words are slurred and go way back in her throat and keeps sounding.

A lump comes in my throat and tears stand in my eyes as I strain to answer. But her eyes close again and she is asleep. We stand silently. After a while we walk out of the room.

She remembers me. There's hope! I feel like there's been a reprieve from the sentence of doom. She's going to be all right. I can't believe she called my name.

In the hall I look around and see a large-boned woman in a wheel chair. She shouts, "I have to go to the baffroom!" The last word seems to hit the wall near me. Startled, I trot quickly through the lobby and hurry to catch up with Dad and Mom.

The sun has gone down as we drive by the school and through our subdivision in North Woods. "Wow!" I say, half to myself. "Auntie may be doing better than we thought, huh?"

Dad turns and gives me a wink. "That was priceless, buddy."

That night we go to prayer meeting. Church on Sunday night is a tradition in our family. Afterwards, I stand around with some of the guys. I'm new so we don't have much to say to each other. I listen to Mrs. McGuire talk about how much trouble Mrs. Whitmire, has as director of the nursing home. "Those old folks just complain day and night," she says. "Say they're lonely. But they've got everything in the world there. Everything they could possibly need."

She goes on about the activity programs and I take out my hand-held video game. I carry it for such times as this. Now I stare at the miniature star warrior on the tiny screen. But Mrs. McGuire's words drift into my lazy brain and stick.

CHAPTER 5

The next day I'm at work in the garage right after school. Mom's gone for the week. Aunt Becky may have induced labor, and Mom doesn't expect to be gone for a long time. Dad says we'll need to arrange our schedule so I can go to the nursing home right after school and then come to the shop later into the evenings. I'm trying to tune-out some of the let down feelings I'm having about Aunt Em. Like maybe Aunt Em's not really getting better. At Dad's words I duck my head and groan inwardly as I go back to my scrub work on the big cycle

Dad wants to know about homework and what kind of books I'm reading now?

"I'm still catching up," I tell him. "Still behind on the reading points."

I'm sanding down a big rusty spot on the Harley's right fender. Looks like there's going to be a hole there when the rust comes out, but Dad doesn't pay attention to such things. Says he'll teach me a thing or two about paint and bodywork on this vehicle.

Out of the blue he says we may try out a few of the bikes he's working on, and asks if my old buddy Jonathan might like to come along some evening.

I stop long enough that he knows something is wrong and that's when the whole sorry mess comes pouring out. At least I'm not blubbering, but I hadn't wanted to tell him.

Dad is quiet for a while. He stops working on the motor casing and studies me for a moment. "Scott, son, I used to have a lot of trouble with my temper too-"

"I was not the one that started it!" Tears sting behind my eyes and I clench my jaw. How can he be so deaf, dumb and blind after all I've told him!

"That's not what I mean son." He sighs and studies me for a moment. "A person can be at fault for giving in to the meanness that other folks dish out, sometimes. What I'm tryin' to say is, that most of the time it's probably best to try to ignore that kind of foolishness."

I stand straight up; slam down sanding papers and rag and glare at him. "Don't you understand? They were makin' fun of *you*, Dad!" I can feel my face flush with anger. How come he is so cool and calm. "They were makin' fun of me when they were makin' fun of you Dad!" I can feel myself about to lose it like a big baby.

He comes over and puts his arm around my shoulders, and I fight off a hiccupping sob. "I know, son. And that's the worst of all this business." Now, I'm really crying. And he wraps his big arms around me in a bear hug.

I pull back after a minute. "Sorry, Dad." I walk back over to the Harley and stare at it.

"Tell you something, Scott. When I went to prison I was madder'n anybody you could name. It wasn't my fault, I said. I was set-up, I said; and a lot of other things. But the bottom line is, I was responsible. I was hooked up with a shady bunch trying to drive a little business into the cycle shop. And I let you and your Mom down. I wasn't thinking straight, and I ended up in a place I'd never have imagined myself going. Not in a million years." He's sitting back on the low stool with his arms across the faded out knees of his Wrangler jeans. His mind seems to drift off just for a moment. Then his gray eyes loose their far away look. "I took a class for anger management in prison. Didn't have to. Just thought it might have something to tell an old bandit like myself." He grins at me.

"Did it?" I grin back; then squat down with my sandpaper to work on the back fender.

"Yes, it did son. In fact, it taught me a lot that I can teach my thirteen-year-old son." I turn my back on him as I feel my lips curl.

"Forget it, Dad! Jonathan's turned into a jerk, and we'll never be friends again."

"Well, if that's what you've decided, Scott. It's up to you son." Dad sounds kind of unconcerned about it, like he's really leaving it up to me.

34

What a relief, I sigh and go back to my sanding. In a way I wish Dad could be right. I mean, say I walk up to Jonathan and say, "Let's let by-gones be by-gones." I shake my head. Somehow this picture does not look possible for me or for him. Besides, there's still the question of Brittany. Let's face it. We both are going out with her. Which one of us does she care about most?

That's a no-brainer question. The answer is, it's the one with the cell phone and roller blades! I give one good hard scrub to the Harley's fender. The metal's so thin I can feel the beginnings of a hole under my finger. I pitch the sand paper in a bucket hooked on the wall by Dad's electric sander.

It's getting on towards dusk outside when Dad and I start finishing up for the day. He's on the phone to Lynn Colliers from the bank. It's about the note being late this month. I can expect to hear a lot of that from now on. I stare out the window. It's too late to go by Rudy's and pitch a few balls. And— I'm ashamed of myself for thinking this—it's also too late to visit Aunt Em this evening. Dad seems to have reached an agreement with Lynn Colliers and in a few minutes we are locking up and walking out. Either Dad senses my mood or feels about like I do and doesn't care to give his feelings any headway by bringing them up. He doesn't talk and neither do I.

Supper is a super-sized can of Ravioli he's heated up I've taken to drinking iced tea, and I put ice in the plastic glasses and mix up some instant tea in a pitcher. We sit down and stare at each other for a moment across the vinyl table-top. It's a friendly look he gives me and it causes me to duck my head, maybe a little out of shame for being so carried away with everything that happens. Dad bows his head too, and we both thank God for the Ravioli and the tea. We don't add, "and for this beautiful day" as Mom always does. I guess neither of us feels that good about how things are going!

I break our silence again with a question. "So how long do you think it'll be before we get the old Harley up and going? And all spiffy-like?" I ask this between bites of my second helping of Ravioli. I wipe orange sauce off my mouth as I watch Dad's face.

He's pushed back the cereal bowl he's been eating out of. Now he gets up and walks over to the sink with it, and swipes a few turns around it with the dish-mop and puts it in the drain basket. He comes back to his tea, swiping around his area with his paper napkin and finally looks at me. "It looks good son. I'm real happy with the way it's coming along." He leans back and takes a long drink of tea. "You know the last time we started up the motor it was getting a miss in it. May be the spark plugs." He gets rid of a piece of ice in his mouth. "We'll check on that tomorrow. We're getting real close, son. Real close. And," He winks at me. "It won't be long till you can start going to practice again. And work in the shop nights and Saturdays. Sound good?"

I grin. It sounds great!

* * *

Next day I'm feeling better about life in general as they say. Course, I've pretty much always been happy about school. It's where all the people you hang with are. I have lunch with the pre-algebra guys, like we're all in this together. They gripe a lot about it and mostly I listen and chow-down on my daily pizza. Today, I'm having green peppers on it. Mom always says she worries that I don't seem to eat any vegetables. Well today I mention something about extra toppings to Mrs. Calaway—the snack-bar lady. We wave to her mornings when she walks to the outside cafeteria tables for a smoking break. She looks like a naughty overgrown kid out there, and I guess we like her for it. Anyway, I'm half joking about getting something extra; picking, like she does with me. Then she hauls off and throws in some of her salad fixings. "Here ye go, slugger."

She's called me that name since I was a little kid. She scoops up a gloved handful of peppers and offers sour cream but I wave her off. Actually they taste pretty good with the cheese and crust. As usual I wolf down the pizza and go away hungry. There must be something to what Mom's always saying about not eating so fast that you overeat. Course there's not a problem with that happening on my school lunch.

After lunch there's a kind of lull where the rest of the junior high kids head for the playground. Some of the guys find a girlfriend or someone to talk with while the other kids do their running around and chasing or whatever. Most of all we just try to show how cool we are; that's why guys look like they're playing a game of chase. We want to show some style and get a girl we've had our eyes on to look at us.

All guys don't fit into this little show we put on. Take Rudy for example.

He just wouldn't know how to begin. He may be what they call a late bloomer. I guess it's pretty much a plateful for him to work on his throwing arm so he can make the team sometime during junior high. Well, I'm beginning to think I don't fit into the little show anymore either.

The guys speak and give me thumbs up still, and Brittany says "Hey Scott," when I walk out of reading class. But somehow, I'm just feeling different about things, I guess. So when Rudy walks up and asks if I want help to start on my Social Studies project, I agree.

My Alamo Chapel is the only one left on the ledge above the worktable in Mr. Ingstrom's classroom. Every year, I'm told, his students have a hands-on project for a grade in junior high. Eighth grade studies Texas history and my assignment is the Alamo. So far my project is still a humongous block of clay that was on my school supplies list for this class. I don't see how I'm supposed to turn *that* into an adobe chapel, but I'm sure Mom could.

But, it looks like this is another one of those things that's up to me, and Rudy maybe. He *did* his already; it's an 1850s period model of a log house, now on display in the upper windows over the hall. An A+, if I ever saw one. I open up the baggie and take out the earth-tone clay and mess with it. I don't have a clue about where to start. The stuff is like a brick already. Then Rudy has this bright idea. "Let's make a drawing! Like an architect does before work gets started on some important building. Got to have a plan, Scott."

By the time the fifth period bell rings I have a pretty good drawing of the Alamo and a feeling for how the clay might be likely to turn into good adobe bricks. I'm going to enjoy this project after all, I've decided. "Thanks Buddy," I say to Rudy, and give him a friendly thump on the shoulder.

"No problem, Bro." He gives me that froggy look from behind his thick glasses and a goofy smile where only one side of his mouth seems to grin.

"Listen, what do you say to taking a bike ride out to the nursing home with me today?"

He stops dead in his tracks although we've both got to hustle to get to fifth period before the last bell rings. "I don't like nursing homes," he says.

"Oh come on. It's not so bad," I lie.

"It's bad," he shakes his head at me, then asks. "At five o'clock you mean?" I nod and we walk on. Then he says, "I can do that." He heads off to his class then turns and shouts. "Meet you by the road after ball practice!"

* * *

Ridgeview Point Convalescent Home is on a small hill. Seems like they call everything around here a point of some kind. It's a long mile or two for me to go from the shop, but for Rudy it's a quick bike ride from the school. I see Coach at the plate, and it looks like practice is still going on, but Rudy meets me already on his bike by the road. Some of the guys wave as we ride off. It's pretty warm and my T-shirt is soaked with sweat.

By the time we get to the top of the small hill Rudy's puffing like he's way bad out of shape. The nursing home is a relic from thirty years ago, but somebody does regular yard work. All kinds of blooming shrubs kick up a riot of pinks and oranges under the old Loblolly Pine trees. We park our bikes and walk inside quickly, like we've got to trick ourselves; or else we might back out and sneak off, instead of going inside.

The wide lobby is almost empty except for one old lady sitting up real close to a big TV. In the adjacent dining room, several tables are already filled up with old folks, waiting on supper. We pass a large boned woman with snowy hair who I suddenly recognize. She catches my eye and we stare at each other till Rudy and I reach the corner. He's crouched down behind me like he's afraid of something. I almost laugh when all of a sudden this big voice booms out of the woman. She's directing it at us, but it doesn't feel like we're being talked to. "M' name's 'Sista,'" she shouts.

We race for the corner, and both duck as if we're being shot at. We stand with our backs to the wall. I'm glad its empty and none of the employees are around to see us acting like idiots. After a minute we walk on down the hall to Aunt Em's room.

I stand close to the bed and stare down at her. She's so still, and I watch her chest rise in fall and feel relieved she's breathing. Rudy sits in a chair near the door, looking out every few seconds as if he's expecting someone. I come around the opposite side of the bed to look at her. She opens her eyes for a moment and looks vague and closes them again. Her stiff hair falls over her damp forehead and her face reminds me of pale cookie dough. She stares at me when I call her name. I unzip my backpack, take out the King James version of the Bible and pull up a chair next to her.

"Oh no, Man. You didn't say nothing about that!"

"Come on, Rudy. It's one chapter. Pipe down." He twists his mouth sideways and looks resigned. "Besides," I continue, "If you were lying here like Auntie and you knew the God who made the universe, wouldn't you want to hear from him about now?"

Rudy frowns at me and seems to dismiss whatever mood he decides I'm in. As for me I'm really speaking for Auntie's benefit. It's what she used to call "sharing the faith." I start in the first chapter of the New Testament and read all those tongue-twisting begats and begottens. Rudy rolls his eyes at me. Aunt Em looks up at me when I say "Abraham" and again at the end when I say "Jesus." But that's all the communicating she does with us.

As we walk back down the hall and turn the corner, Sista is shouting. She seems not to notice us and I stop for a moment, and not meaning to, I stare at her miniature hand. She has twisted it under her chin and it reminds me of a tiny bird wing. The gesture makes her look vulnerable. I feel a familiar pressure behind my nose like I'm near to crying. Without really thinking about it I bend my head down and plant a peck of a kiss on her snow-topped head.

Rudy thinks it's a hoot, and we both double over laughing when we get outside. It was a goofy joke to Rudy. I'm not sure it was a joke to me.

CHAPTER 6

A dream wakes me up in the early early morning. I don't dream often; at least not where I can remember what I dreamed. It's odd that I didn't dream about Sista—and all that squirrely hollering she was doing. But no, I dream I'm four-years old again and Auntie is reading to me in our favorite window seat, just like it was so long ago. Lying here I'm not sure how the old childhood story got in my mind.

Did I dream or just remember it?

It's the story of *The Velveteen Rabbit* by Margery Williams. The storybook boy has so many toys that his old Nanny just puts his new stuffed toy in a cabinet for some later time. I used to ask Auntie to read the story real often. I liked to hear it over and over again. In the dream I hear that old Skin Horse again. He's talking to the Rabbit in Auntie's mimicry. "You become 'real' when someone loves you," he says. To me this is a message from Auntie. I know I must find a way to help her get her life back. She's not that old, I tell myself.

I'm sitting up in bed now. It's still dark outside, and I know without looking at my alarm clock that it's about three o'clock in the morning. I'm trying to think of how many years old Auntie must be. Sixty something? Uncle Hugh is the oldest. I snap my fingers. That's it! I go down the hall and prowl around in the alcove looking for our phone book. I'll still have to wait for daylight, at least, but I feel sure that Uncle Hugh will help me.

Much later, I'm still lying in bed when the phone rings and I hear Dad pick it up. I can tell he's just woke up even though he says "Good morning" like he's been up for hours. Idly, I lay there listening to their conversation. Odd, I've never thought about it before, but Dad and Uncle Hugh don't like each other. Also, I'm thinking that Dad's always known this. It's something he's known and takes in stride. Sort of like, it's Uncle's own business if he doesn't choose to like Dad. Funny, how well I'm beginning to understand Dad. Like right now I already know his answer to my question as to why Uncle doesn't like him. "Now Scott," he'll say, "listen to me son. Everybody doesn't have to like me. Fact, I don't even expect them to. And you know what else," I seem to hear him say. "You shouldn't expect everyone to like you, because they won't."

My conversation with Uncle Hugh is good. He's kind of tickled about my idea, and for some reason he asks if I plan to be a doctor maybe. I'm shocked and say "no way! I'm going to play baseball." He almost shouts with laughter into the telephone and I pull it back from my ear.

"Got to do something they'll pay you for boy. You might want to play baseball as a hobby. Course some people have..." His voice trails off like he's lost interest in his own words. "Harumph," I hear him clearing his throat on the other end of the line. "Okay boy, you get with this Dr. Barnard fellow. He's the staff doctor at that convalescent home. You see what he says about all this. If he thinks it'll work, we'll sure do her."

I'm about to ask him if he doesn't know I'm only thirteen and that maybe the doctor won't even talk to me anyway. Then Uncle goes off on another tangent. "Boy, you still have that attack dog?" I don't say anything since I don't know what he's talking about anyway. "That dachhound, weiner-dog?" He doesn't wait for me to answer, but just goes on; though I do remember now. The little dog had been run over near the mailbox one day. Aunt and I didn't talk about it, because she'd felt so bad about it. It was seven or eight years ago.

Aunt Em and I were drinking lemonade slushies on the back patio when Uncle Hugh had come to visit. He'd said "Hello, the house!" and stepped out on the patio. Hank, the dachhound, came from behind the swing like a ferret and made a dash for Uncle's ankles. We'd giggled about it for a long time, because Uncle had looked so funny trying to get away from the dog. He said that little pup had chewed the cuffs off one of his trouser legs. Remembering the time so long ago makes me feel good. Maybe things are not so bad. Maybe Aunt can get well again.

* * *

It is stupid to get up so early and be late for school. It's almost seven forty-five and my first class at school starts just a few minutes after eight. I grin at Dad and holler "Good morning;" deciding to skip the shower. I jump into my clothes. I feel lightheaded from lack of sleep, but happy, like a load has been lifted from my shoulders. Uncle agreed that Aunt can have physical therapy, and that he'll have the doc put her with a special trainer who'll come every afternoon and work with her if the doctor thinks that will be best. Dad promises to call the doctor and schedule a visit sometime after school. I'm happier than I've been in a long time as I jump on my bike, shoot away down the driveway and pedal off to school.

The guys have learned about my nursing home visits, thanks to Mrs. Cronin. This morning she tells the class what a good citizen I am. I duck my head and try to hide, like I'm taking a sudden interest in my library book. I'm nailed anyway.

Everyone giggles and Brittany wiggles her eyebrows and grins at me. Mrs. Cronin is not about to shut up about it either, and I can feel my face getting hot. "Our Scott's been reading to shut-ins at the nursing home." Mrs. Cronin says.

I turn around and give Rudy a puzzled look. He looks puzzled himself and shoves out his lips and shrugs an "I don't know who told her this, but it wasn't me," look. I turn back around and everyone is clapping. "Speech, speech!" Dan Fowler sticks both thumbs in the air, and the clapping continues.

Hoping this will stop soon, I get out of my seat, crouch along the floor in a break dance routine and pop up again, spread my arms and take a bow in both directions across the room.

"Way to go, Scott-ee! Jonathan's voice booms in a silly guffaw above the clapping and giggles. "You sure can do some stuff!" He's grinning like he thinks he's Eddie Murphy. I grin back at him and join the fun. What else can I do?

* * *

That evening in the shop Dad and I work on grouting-in and building up the thin and worn-through places on the Harley's fenders. I watch as he takes a dab of grout, works it into the worn metal, then rubs and sands it down to form a bond. I take fine sand paper and fine tune the work of the big sander. Dad does another inspection, rubbing his fingers along the new material to check for imperfections.

This work is slow and it gives you a muscle cramp in your shoulders. But we've got a big part of it done by quitting time. Our next big job will be to strip off the cycle's chrome and do some taping to get the Harley ready for paint.

We talk about school, and I decide to tell him about the incident. He looks pleased, but doesn't say much. Just that I'll have to learn whose opinions about who I am matter most to me—mine or other peoples'.

I knock off early to get to Dr. Bernard's office before closing time. As I start out the door Dad yells at me. "Hey Scott, let *me* see that break dance routine of yours!" I grin back at him, and he says the neatest thing. "I'm glad you're my son, Scott."

CHAPTER 7

Dr. Barnard's office is a short bike ride past the hardware store, tucked away in a little cul de sac. It looked like a relic from the past, a lot like the doctor himself.

He doesn't look as busy as he said. But he can give me a few minutes, he says. And he's "always glad to see young people take an interest in the medical field." I apologize for taking up his time but don't feel like he was being taken away from anything. After all, an umbrella and stuff is by the door and his part time secretary, old Mrs. McElroy, is waving goodbye as she heads back for her purse.

In a while the doctor stops puttering around and walks up to me and sits down across from me. He's an older guy who looks like he doesn't get a regular haircut and he has bushy eyebrows that need a trim. "So, what did you want to talk about?" I've given him a list of questions and he picks up the paper and stares at it for a few minutes. Then he stares at me with interest. "You're Emma Oakdale's boy." It isn't a question.

"Uh, no sir. I'm her grandson. Not grandson though. She's my Mom's great aunt. But—" I swallow here and wish he'd not stare. He isn't being unfriendly, just an old guy who isn't even thinking about me, I guess. "I mean, she's always been my—grandma." I finish lamely, and almost tell him Auntie is my forever friend. Instead, I open my eyes wide and stare back at him to hide my feelings. He thumps me on the shoulder, a sign of affection, I guess.

He walks over to the secretary's desk, taps a few keys on the keyboard and snorts and shakes his head. "Where's old McE when I need her?" I ask if I can help.

He shakes his head and walks over to the file cabinets and starts pulling out files. "These are
old vertical files, but way to treat a stroke don't change an awful lot." He rubs his hand across his mouth thoughtfully, motions me to a chair and opens the files between us. He really does plan to give me some time. I'm impressed.

The papers are about recovery statistics for stroke and how to help stroke victims. After a while he closes the folder and says. "We don't know how things will turn out Scott. There is not a way to predict such things. Except," and he looks pained; "there's often a second stroke and sometimes a third."

He waits while I stare at him. I swallow several times and try to say something but fail.

He shakes his head in sympathy with me. "And what can you do, Scott?" He shakes his head and sighs. "Well, here's what you do." Putting a hand on my shoulder, he gives my shoulder a pat, then stands up. Guess that means it's time for me to go. "You can keep doing what you're doing. Yes sir. What you've been doing helps." He rubs his hand over his chin like he's checking for whiskers. "You keep it up. Visiting, reading to her and trying to get her to talk to you are the best things you can do. I'll talk to Hugh Oakdale and we'll set up times for the therapist to come and work with your Aunt."

We shake hands, and I thank him for spending time to help me. "And, Scott" His voice stops me at the door. "Don't worry so much. Things have a way of working out." He shakes his head as if speaking half to himself as he shuffles some papers on the desk. "They may not always suit us; and we may not always understand why things happen the way they do." Then he looks up at me and adds. "Sometimes people recover from stroke and live many productive years after. Why don't we expect that for Emma?"

I grin my agreement. And yell "thanks again" as I head out the door.

I'm running late for the nursing home again. It seems late because I've started thinking that since they eat their dinner at five o'clock there's not much left of the evening.

When I come by the school, the baseball practice hasn't broken up yet; but Rudy gives me a wave and heads out to the road to meet me. He swings up his backpack that he has stashed under the jasmine vines, climbs on his bike and we take off down the highway for the short bike ride.

We sneak through the empty lobby. Almost all the old folks must be in the dining room. "Oh rats! We missed Sista." Rudy whispers to me as we walk past glass doors. Aunt is sleeping when we walk in. Rudy takes up his usual spot on the side near the door, like he can't wait to leave. He looks at me and out the door every so often like he wants to know if it's safe. Guess he thinks Sista will come and attack us.

A young nurse, who looks like a high school volunteer, comes in and takes Aunt's pulse and blood pressure. She asks if Rudy and I are some of Aunt's kin. Rudy thinks the nurse is cute and he gives me a high five sign. She turns to look at him and we try to look innocent. She doesn't seem to notice and instead looks at the Bible I've taken out of my backpack. Now she nods towards it. "Does she understand you, or acknowledge you at all?"

"So far, no; but we keep hoping."

She turns at the door and looks at me like I've said something awfully intelligent. Then she nods, wiggles her hand in a little wave and disappears out the door. Rudy grates his teeth together in mock pain. "I think I'm in love." He doubles over and rocks back and forth for a minute. I roll my eyes toward the ceiling. Rudy's becoming a real joker.

I clear my throat meaningfully and sit down on the other side of Auntie. She's still sleeping, but I've made up my mind to read or talk to her. Anyway, I tell Rudy, who doesn't understand why we'd read to or talk to someone who's not responsive; it's doctor's orders. He shakes his head back and forth like I've lost it, and there's no hope for me.

I open the Bible to Matthew three in the New Testament and recognize it's about John the Baptist. After I've read a few verses I get to the part about what kind of person John was. I stop and begin to describe John. I know the story from having heard it so many times. "His mother knew he would be a different kind of person because God's spirit spoke to her and her husband. Sure enough John went to live in the wilds of Judea. Everybody thought he was a wild man!"

Aunt hasn't stirred at all. And so far I've been entertaining Rudy. "John's clothes were made out of camel hair, and he wore a leather girdle about his loins; he ate grasshoppers and he ate wild honey. But he had a message to bring."

I look at Aunt and her eyes open. She stares at me as like we're having a conversation. Her lips move and she looks like she has something she wants to tell me. Then she gives up and smiles without opening her mouth.

I lean toward her white face, and my eyes get blurry. "The message was that the Messiah was coming, Aunt!" She gives the smallest nod. In spite of myself, a tear drops right on her face. She flinches like she's had a small shock; then her face goes rigid and she closes her eyes again.

I drop my head down and would have had a real boo-hoo session if Rudy hadn't been there. Instead, I kiss Auntie on the forehead, and lay my cheek against her hair for a small moment. Then Rudy and I get up and walk quietly outside.

CHAPTER 8

We walk outside and it seems strange that the sun hasn't set yet. I feel like I've been set back in time. I can't help but think how I need to shake off the gloom that's set in. Aunt Em is not lost yet. Dr. Barnard told me to expect ups and downs. My problem is that I expected so much when Aunt woke up for a minute. Or was it even a minute? The point is that Auntie *had* woke up, even though it was for such a little minute. *This* is good news. I'm telling myself these things as Rudy and I are pedaling back.

"There'll be an hour or two before it gets dark," Rudy is saying. "Are you done in the cycle shop?"

I know what he's thinking. I nod. "Want to stop by the baseball field?" This idea breaks like a shot of adrenalin, and we pedal faster.

Rudy swoops down and grabs his backpack from the jasmine shrubs near the road. And I look above the vines to see that we're not alone. In the field a bunch of guys are catching; and several, including my friend Jonathan, are latched onto the fence near the entry gate. I start to smile, and pull my bike in near the fence. The guys don't seem friendly, but it could be just me, I think.

Rudy doesn't seem to notice as he swings his backpack onto his shoulders and stares at them with a crooked smile. "Hey guys. What's up?"

Jonathan grins and they all start to laugh and we join them. Then a few more of the guys from the field come trotting up and hang onto the fence with them.

"How's it going?" I say.

"So, so." Jonathan answers. He turns and looks at the other guys with a

48

silly grin, then turns back to me. "How's the motorcycle business going?"

I start to smile. Before I can answer one of the guys says, "Yeah! How's the cycle business going?"

I grin. "Not bad. In fact I'm—"

"Hey, you still working on them old junkers?"

I bristle and clench my fist. My face gets hot. "What's it *to* you, Jerk?

They all laugh. Rudy's got his fists clenched too. And I just wish he were not here. It seems wrong to have him involved in the fight. I seem to hear Dad saying, "Walk away, Scott." So I give Rudy a nod and turn my bike around.

One of the guys jumps on top of the chain link fence and starts to crow like a rooster. Everybody laughs again. And they start waving their arms and pretending to scale the fence like they're trying to escape. Really stupid guys, I'm thinking as we start to pedal off. Mostly spoiled brats who've never had to do much of anything to earn their keep.

I halfway grin to myself. About like I was before I learned that lots of things aren't going my way. I don't even mind working in the shop now, but I don't know how I may feel about it later when the guys start the season and I'm not on the team. I look back at my so-called friends.

Someone shouts, "Oh Warden, but I didn't do it. It was a mistake!" My heart drops in my stomach. Again the voice trails after us, "Help me, help me!" And I know I won't be able to let this pass. But what to do? We stop our bikes and I look at Rudy. Now we stare at the hillside with its scattering of small pellet-sized rocks. We grin at each other.

"Not much to do battle with," Rudy grins. "But we can't complain about lack of ammunition!"

We junk the bikes in the ditch, mount the hillside and start pelting away. Rudy's aim is a little off, as usual. But we can hear pings where the little rocks hit the fence, and it looks like the guys are getting the point. They start to run back to the field and we keep pelting away, hoping they don't decide to break through the rain of rocks and come toward us.

We fall back exhausted and start to giggle as foolishly as our mockers did a few minutes ago. A white SUV comes down the road toward us; slows and pulls in the gate at the field. I scoot down to my bike with an eye still on the SUV. Rudy and I scramble for our stuff and pedal our heads off trying to get out of sight before the kids start driving by with their parents.

It's not that we're scared we've done something wrong, I tell myself. Rudy reads my thoughts. He's huffing and panting as we swing into a grassy lane behind the library and dance studio. "Scott," Rudy calls after me as we stop. He takes off his baseball cap and swipes his forehead with the back of his arm. "You think we'll catch Ned for this?"

I've got a nagging worry about it, especially since we started running off like we did. Though it seemed like a logical thing to answer the guys with a whole slough of rocks, now things could go bad with our parents, not to mention theirs. Then, who knows what kind of lies the guys will tell to make themselves look good. We would catch it, of that I was sure. I shake my head at Rudy in resignation. "You can count on it Dude."

"What do you think they'll do to us?" Rudy stares down at the handlebars on his bike.

"Kill us, I expect." Rudy looks at me quickly, and the humor of it strikes me like it's not happening to us, but somebody else. That's when I start to laugh and Rudy joins in. We laugh at our silly selves and the stupid guys running back towards the dugout. We fall off our bikes laughing, lying on our backs looking up at the tall pines above the grassy lane.

Not much time could have passed, but it's almost dusk when we ride back into our part of town. "Look Rudy," I say, as he starts to turn into his driveway. "If you don't want to hang around with me, it's okay. I won't feel like you're disloyal if you don't want to be friends or hang out with me anymore."

Rudy grins his lopsided grin, cocks his head and gives me a frog stare. "Scott, I've taken lots of razzing about my name, since I was a little kid. I can tell how you feel, well, sort of. So, guess I'll stick around." He turns into his driveway then stops and adds. "Besides, that's the most fun I've had all day, Dude," he laughs.

.Dad's on the phone when I walk inside. He nods towards the kitchen and says, "Stir the spaghetti, Scott." He's getting ready to hang up now. "I know, Lid. You give her my love. And I love you too honey."

I lower the flame under the saucepan. Stir a little and taste it, realizing suddenly how starved I am. Dad's other specialty is stew. Though most of the time we heat up canned soup, fry Spam sandwiches or open up cans of pork and beans.

Now Dad calls from the hall. "Come say hi, Scott."

Turns our Aunt Becky has a disease called Lupus. Too bad I say, I could have asked Dr. Barnard about that today. Dad sort of holds up the wall and listens while I tell Mom what the doctor said.

Mom asks about school and for some reason she wants to know how things are going with my friends. I tell her Rudy is helping with my Social Studies project.

"Oh, is he the boy you do pitching with in his front yard?"

"Yeah. He's a good guy, Mom."

"I know, I know, son." She's quiet for a minute and I'm kind of puzzled. Then she asks, "So how is your old friend, Jonathan?"

She hardly gets the words out before I answer. "He's a jerk Mom! You wouldn't believe what he did-" I stop just before I tell her about the guys mocking me.

"I'm sorry you're having so much trouble with your old friends, Scott" Her voice is gentle, and I blink several times to keep back tears. "You know, son, that's one of the reasons you wanted to come back to Ridge Point. You wanted to be with Jonathan and Dan and the fellows." I don't say anything and after a moment she adds. "Well, things can change son. People change and it could still work out for you."

I mumble something like "Yeah, sure."

Thankfully, she changes the subject. "Okay son, tell me about our favorite subject, Aunt Emma."

I go on for a while about my visit to see Aunt Em today. She and Dad are thrilled and say they're really proud of me. I can't help but wonder how proud they'll be after they hear about the rock throwing battle today. Now, I decide there's no real reason to tell them anyway.

* * *

The next morning Rudy still has this on his mind. He calls first thing and starts talking about it. He wonders if Coach Gerrard might find out what happened. Rudy is worried that he might get thrown off the team for rock throwing. I tell him I don't know. But I sure hope not.

I'm leaving late for class again this morning. Dad tells me to go to baseball practice just as I start out the door. I think I've misunderstood, but he says he's got a meeting at 3:30 and he figures it'll take about an hour or so. I wait until he comes in the room, like I can't believe it.

I can't.

He's drying his hair off from the shower and he comes over and thumps me on the shoulder playfully. "Believe it Buddy! Now better get a move on or you'll be late for sure."

I walk into reading class and Mrs. Cronin stares at me until I sit down. The guys all just look up at me and then go back to their reading. Funny how I've just discovered I've forgotten and left my backpack. I give Rudy a thumbs up, and search around for something to read, all the while wondering where I could have left my backpack. Now, I remember it's at the shop.

I sigh heavier than I mean to, and Mrs. Cronin looks up over her glasses at me. "Scott, do you have a problem, this morning?" Someone murmurs something and everyone laughs. She asks what they said. Justin Bean says that he guesses I'm thinking about "citizenship" and being a good citizen and all that kind of thing." Mrs. Cronin looks puzzled, but everyone else thinks that's funny too. So they all laugh again.

Finally they all quiet down and I ask Mrs. Cronin for permission to go to the library. "I forgot my backpack," I say.

On my way back I meet Jonathan and Brittany in the hall. Funny, I get a little twinge of pain looking at them, and I realize that I'm jealous. I grin to cover up my discomfort.

"How's it goin'?" I say and keep walking.

I know things will never work out like Mom says. I've made enemies of all the guys in my old crowd. Then I set my teeth in a grim line. And they've made an enemy of me.

* * *

Before last period is over I get permission to leave a little early to go by the cycle shop and grab my backpack. My baseball glove is still in it. Earlier I almost told Dad I didn't really want to go to baseball practice,, but he'd surely have smelled a rat.

At the shop there's a shiny red car in front and I remember Dad has an appointment. This morning he didn't mention who he was meeting since I was rushing out the door and didn't care. Now I open the door quietly and see Dad and a youngish blonde woman. Both of them are leaning over his makeshift desk. I stare at them for a minute, trying to figure out who she can be.

They don't see me even when I walk in and pick up my backpack. She has put her hand on his arm and looks at him, shaking her head. I hear her say, "Nick," softly.

Dad nods. "I know. But how can I go back on my word?"

I back out the door and ease it closed behind me. My eyes tear up and my chest feels like I've been hit with a bat. "What's *wrong* with him?" I grind my teeth together; stare at the shiny red car, and kick one of the tires. So that's what Dad's up to these days, I whisper bitterly to myself.

* * *

I cross Lakeview Point Road and pedal down Main, make the corner at the library and turn on Ridgepoint Road. My mind's in a time warp. It's a wonder I don't run past the practice field.

Since we've moved back to this town so many things have gone wrong. Sometimes it looks like just nothing can work out right. I turn in at the gate and park my bike. The players are already on the field and I'm glad nobody notices when I walk up.

Anyway, for the first time I'm on the field and not thinking about baseball. Dad's turned into a sneak with some woman he's stringing along. Now the coach will probably run me off.

I'm muttering under my breath like a demented ogre and have about talked myself into turning and running when Coach Gerrrard waves and motions me over to the sidelines for a chat. "Oh brother! Here it comes!" I'm thinking.

In the stands are a scattering of kids and a few parents. I look around but don't see Rudy anywhere. Maybe Coach is about to give me a lecture on how practice works. Instead, he eyes me for a minute, nods towards centerfield, and tosses me a glove as I trot out to play for the Fins. Jonathan is pitching. He stops and watches me for a few seconds, then turns back to throw one right across the plate.

Justin Bean is a good hitter and he knocks a high drive down the middle. The ball whizzes over Jonathan's head, but I reach up and snag it with no sweat. I don't look up but can hear one person clapping from the stands as the Fins trot down to the dugout for our turn at bat.

Justin, the tank, Bean, is coming toward me. Point him in a certain direction and don't get in front of him. I can tell by his face that he intends to flatten me. I dart out of his way and end up walking with Jonathan back to the dugout. I can tell he's watching me from the tail of his eye.

"Hey Bub!" He's talking to me but staring ahead at the stands. "What do you say we have a meeting?" He's talking out of the corner of his mouth and looking like what Rudy would call 'resolute.'

"What's up?" I slow down and look directly at him. "You and the guys planning to have another little gossip session?"

The words are barely out of my mouth, and he swings at me.

Looking back on things I probably shouldn't have ducked; at least then I could have gotten some sympathy out of the deal.

But I did duck, and not a nanosecond too soon.

He's surprised, like he caught himself doing something un-cool.

I grin at him and he looks really sorry; it's the first honest look I've seen from him in a while.

I give him a playful punch on the shoulder to diffuse the situation.

"Can't make it today, Bozo," I smile again, enjoying this. "Catch you later though. Besides maybe you guys can use the time to think up some more nasty gossip."

Jonathan's face is red. He knows we're in trouble as the Coach call us to the sidelines. Everyone goes into slow motion, and the whole field stops and stares at the coach as we walk over to him.

He wags his finger at the hind catcher and pitcher. His beady eyes squint and he looks mean as an angry pig. "Play ball!" he roars at the field.

The field erupts into motion like a frozen picture that suddenly becomes animated. I cut my eyes across at Jonathan to see if he looks as intimidated as I feel.

Now Gerrard's beady eyes size up both of us. He comes alongside us and his red face looks like a volcano as he sneers,. "YOU'RE OFF THE TEAM!"

I glance back at the field to see how this announcement is taking hold. Everyone gives a little jerk like there's been a seismic shock. Then Dan Fowler starts pitching another ball across home plate. It crosses my mind that the coach isn't talking to me. Since I'm not even on the team, the coach's announcement can only be bad news for Jonathan.

This happy thought gets a chill out when the Coach gives me a mincing glare. The angry gremlin is still emoting. "Go sit on the bleachers!"

Startled, we jump and start walking off, thankful to have our heads still attached. "TOGETHER!" He shouts after us.

We flop down several yards apart on the second bleacher. The coach glares a threatening look and we inch a few feet closer. I hear a giggle somewhere above us. Turning around I see Brittany. She waves. Jonathan turns and looks too, but he doesn't acknowledge her. Now I look on past her and can't believe my eyes. It's Dad. I frown at him, puzzled. He frowns back.

I turn back around and stare at the field without really seeing it. "What's *Dad* doing here?" I turn and give him another quick look, just checking to see if he has that blonde woman sitting with him.

Jonathan follows my stare. This time he waves at Brittany, and makes a clicking noise, doing his Eddie Murphy laugh as he looks up at her. I figure this must be for my benefit since Brittany's too far away to hear any of it. Jonathan's such a fool. I can see Brittany's big possum grin coming back at him, so I guess he's doing all right for a fool.

He inches closer to me now, like we're just pals after all. I watch him like he might be a rabid dog. "Scott-ee." He bites off the word like it something to get rid of quick.

Before Jonathan can say anything else, the Coach calls time. We stand up to leave, but coach catches our eye across the field and motions us to sit back down. The rest of the parents in the stand sit down too. The outfielders walk back to the dugout, take off their helmets and start to put away their bats and gear. Jonathan leans closer. "Meet you behind the library after this is over."

CHAPTER 9

Jonathan and I are sitting there and minding our own business. At least he's moved back over to his spot on the bleachers. The Coach trots over, wags a finger toward the parents left in the stands and Dan Fowler's Dad and Mom, Rudy's Mom and Pop Weaver, Jonathan's grandpa walk over. They sit down in front of us. Dad and Brittany come down the bleachers together. She takes a seat beside Jonathan, and Dad comes over and sits beside me. I look at him, but he doesn't look friendly. So I turn back to look at the coach. He's calmed down.

He folds his arms and plants his stout legs apart, tucks in his head and pucks out his lips. We're getting the full treatment of Coach's version of the bad cop. I almost think he's going to spout off a line from the latest UIL play. If only he would. But I know what was coming. I look around for Rudy and catch his mom's eye as she stares me down.

"We've got a problem," Coach begins. "These two boys here;" he wags a finger at Jonathan and I. He shakes his head from side to side and purses his lips. "You know, I'd of thought they was buddies. I mean from all I can see. But now—" He shakes his head again and stares at us. "This is hard for me to believe about you fellows—"

"Not for some of us!" It's Rudy's Mom. "And it looks like you don't know what's been going on, Coach. They've been having rock battles out there." She pokes the air towards the front gate with a bronzed finger. "That's right!" she is almost hollering at him, like she's answering some question he asked. I duck my head. Poor Rudy; it's a pity he has a hawk like that for a Mom. No wonder he was afraid to trip over the begonias.

Coach is intrigued. No one says anything for a long few seconds. We are having a staring match. Dad's watching me. Jonathan's cutting his eyes at me but still looking at the coach, and coach is staring at all of us.

Dad speaks first and startles me. "Tell us what you know about this Scott. It seems like some of the folks think you know." He gives me a nudge. "How about it son? What do you know about this business?"

"Can't say Dad."

I can feel his eyes on me. I duck my head further and avoid looking at him. Not that I care about what he thinks anymore. The big sneak. Why should I tell him about something *I've* done wrong. And I don't care what the rest of them do either.

Coach gives up on the blame session. He winds things up by telling Jonathan he's off the team for the game this week, and maybe from now on.

We all get up to leave and he says to me, "Don't bother coming back to practice with us again, buddy."

"You bet!" I answer.

"Hey!" He shouts and I turn around. "Don't smart off to me, you hear me boy?"

Dad steps back alongside the Coach. "See here, Coach." Dad can have steel in his eyes and still talk soft. "Scott may know something about this. I expect he does. I *will* find out one way or another." He looked like he was about to walk off and then turned back to Coach. "But you keep a civil tongue in your head when you're talking to my son."

I almost laugh out loud, even though I'm sure the parents will think Dad's being a wise guy. What do I care? I shrug again.

"You bet, buddy—ah…Mr. Gully." Coach looks sheepish. Probably he won't let me forget this. Course I won't be around the baseball field anymore, I remind myself as Dad and I walk back to the jeep.

I tell Dad I've got some unfinished business to tend to and we eye each other for a moment. Finally he nods and gets in the jeep.

Watching Dad drive off now I've just decided not to go meet Jonathan, after all. It's not a good day for a fight, much as I've been telling myself that I need to give Jonathan a good walloping. Right now, I need to see Aunt Em. Somehow I know that things will be all right if I can just talk to her for a little while.

It's late to visit. The old folks have already gone from the dining room and I can hear a TV blaring in one wing of the hall. I turn the corner from the lobby and there's Sista in her usual spot. But it looks like everyone else has retired for the evening. That's okay with me. There's only one person here who matters to me.

Aunt Em is asleep too. She doesn't respond when I nudge her and talk loud in her ear. She just lays there, her gray streaked hair framing a pasty white face. Her mouth is shut firm like she's just made up her mind to something or other. Suddenly that makes me pucker up like I'm going to cry. I sit and stare at her for a long while; and suddenly I start telling her about the first time we went fishing in the lake.

She'd helped me bait my hook and the tiny minnow escaped. He kept tickling my hands and she finally speared him through the tail and onto my fishing hook. I watch Aunt's face now, but there's no change and I go on to repeat her favorite story about manners. "Remember?" I say. "You told me that I need to say 'Yes'm and No'm' because that's good manners." I lean closer to the bed. "Do you remember what you said I told you?"

I go on talking just like she knows what I'm saying. "I told you the 'minnows' died! Remember Aunt?"

I'm pleading now. "Please get well Aunt Em. I'm so lost without you. Dad's got a girlfriend, I think. I'm thrown off the team. Course I've never been on it anyway. Jonathan wants to meet me, so we can fight." I droop my head down on the bed and sob out my pain and hopeless feeling for Aunt's deaf years. As I raise my head I catch sight of a floral housecoat and white head as a wheelchair passes by the door.

In the lobby Sista puts out her bird wing hand. It reminds me of a seal. I stop beside her and wait, suddenly realizing she's been by Aunt's room. Just nosey, I guess; or lonely; like a lot of the old folks here.

"Your Aunt can' hep' you anymore, YOUNG MAN!"

I jump back and glare at her, I hope.

"She's—" Sista speaks with a struggle and seems to use all her energy to get out the words. "She's GONE—"

She tries to stop me as I move away. "She's going to a BETTER PLACE!"

My face burns hot. What does this old witch know, I'm thinking. I brush off the bird wing. In spite of myself I start spouting off. "It's none of your business old woman." I start to walk off.

Her big voice follows me. "But she knows how you feel anyway, BOY!"

I stop for a moment, but I'm about to break out in another bucket of tears.

"She KNOWS! She can HEAR!" Sista calls after me, as I hurry out the door to get away from the words.

* * *

I wheel in behind the library. Maybe I *am* in the mood for a fight! But there's nobody there, and the library is closed. Great! So now I'm a coward along with everything else. Tomorrow ought to be a real cool day!

I ride home in the quiet dusk along the street with flowering plants and lighted windows. Behind some I can spot families eating their evening meal. I slip in my house quietly. From the kitchen I hear Dad whistling a toneless song. I make it to my room and lock the door just in case I bust loose in another big boo-ho session. Dad knocks a couple of times and when I don't answer he goes away.

After a while I hear him on the phone, talking to Mom, or maybe to that blonde woman. I think about cracking the door to listen, but decide I don't really care. Too disgusted to study, I toss my books on my worktable, turn out the light and stretch out across my bed. For a long time I just lie here and stare out the window at the streetlight down towards the corner.

I keep lying across the bed, hiccupping and feeling like a dumbbell. I search around for something to feel good about. It's useless.

There was something Brittany once told me about myself. "You know what I like most about you Scott?" That may have been the time we sat in the skating rink and I tore up her wet napkin from her coke. "I like how you're able to laugh and like, you know, mock yourself. When a lot of people would feel sorry for themselves. You laugh!"

That was a joke! If she could see me now, she'd laugh. I've made a mess of everything I've touched. Well, there are a lot of things I couldn't help and not a lot I can do to change the rest of them: Aunt Em's sickness, Dad's treachery and Jonathan egging the guys on me. A few of what Mom calls my self-pity tears start to roll down my face. Now I feel pretty disgusted. Mom was wrong; I couldn't do anything about these problems.

Or can I? I sit up. There *is* something I can do!

Feeling relieved again I finally lie back and before I drift off to sleep, I know that Jonathan and I will have a settling. After we talk, I'm going to punch the jerk's lights out!

* * *

The next day I meet Rudy at our Social Studies work station. When I walk up he's bent over my project, like he's checking it out. "Hey, yo!" I shout.

He jumps half afoot like he's been caught stealing.

"How's it goin'?" I walk over to him and adjust some loose miniatures on my model.

"Looking good." Rudy squares off and studies the model admiringly. "Seriously Scott, this is turning out NICE."

"Thanks Dude. I couldn't have done it without you!" He gives me a thumbs up and I add. "Nice of you to help out."

"So how's your essay doing? So far, I mean?" He's kind of fidgety, and wanders off toward the other side of the room while we talk.

"Bout to finish it," I answer. "Maybe a page to end it and work a little more to get it to a final draft." I stretch; then grab up my baseball and stare at it. "Tomorrow, I think." I toss my baseball back in my pack. "How's about we pitch a few balls after school?"

Rudy nods and clears his throat uncomfortably, like he didn't understand me. "Mom, she got all bent outta shape about the rock-throwing."

Remembering how Rudy's Mom must have started things on a downhill slide for Coach the other day made me want to laugh. "I know." I try not to grin.

The grin is clean wiped off with Rudy's next words. "Then Dad asks 'how old I am.' He reminded me that I got pops for rock-throwing when I was six." He stammers and ducks his head before looking at me again. "Anyway Scott, I'm punished. I can still play ball but I have to stay away from you for a couple of weeks.

"That's your punishment?" I ask

61

"Yeah. Dad says he'll think about whether I can hang out with you after that."

My face kind of freezes up, and I realize how much I've come to depend on Rudy's friendship. "Bummer," I manage to say. It sounds like a croak.

Just then fifth period bell rings and we make a run for class. I've got a sort of gut-wrenching feeling. I can't lose the only friend I have left, can I? No, I decide. I'll just try to play their little game, shrug off the slights and smart Alec remarks.

Before I get to the science lab, Brittany stops me and says, "let's talk." We end up alone in a little alcove near the water coolers. She wants to know why Jonathan and I are going to fight.

"We're—How did you know about it?"

"Oh, word gets around." She digs her nails into my hand. "Don't do it Scott. Don't fight him. It's not going to solve anything."

I bristle. It will solve something for me.

"Jonathan thinks I like you best, and he's jealous." She lets all this out in one big breath and I can see she's embarrassed.

I stare at her. "*Do* you like me best?" I blurt this out and wish I could bite my tongue off.

"Oh yeah. I sure do, best friend."

"Come off it Brittany. Be serious." Looks like I really want to know.

"I *am* serious!" She shoves her elbow in my ribs. "Jonathan does not want me to like you."

"But why?"

"I don't know Scott. Maybe because he was king of the mountain before you came back."

I want to ask her if that means I'm 'king of the mountain' now. But I've not got the nerve to ask it.

I am still wondering about this idea of Brittany's while Carp Swinney, my science partner and I dissect a sheep's heart. Brittany told me another thing too. Jonathan is grounded and he's got his cell phone taken away. His Dad was mad, and he wasn't going to allow Jonathan to play baseball for a while. Well, I'm thinking it's about time someone else has some trouble besides me. Course I'm not exactly broadcasting my troubles like Jonathan is. At this point I'd told Dad exactly nothing about any of these problems. Maybe the one with Jonathan *will* clear up without a fight.

* * *

After school, I wheel my bike in behind the library. I lean it against one of the giant Loblolly Pines, now wondering if Carp Swinney might have forgotten to tell Jonathan to meet me here. I flatten out on the ground and stare up into the treetops where a gray squirrel is clucking and scurrying way up high.

I lean up on one elbow, and see Jonathan pull around the corner. Glad he didn't bring an audience, I get up and watch as he leans his bike near mine. "Hey, Jonathan," I say. "Glad you could make it.

"He ducks his head and sort of curls his lips like he's putting up with some crap. "Yeah, yeah." He stops in front of me. "So, let's get on with it, Scottee!"

I ignore his attitude problem. "Jonathan, I want to talk to you first. You know, tell you some stuff…" I stop for a minute, try to measure his closed angry face. I shrug. "For old times sake, Jonathan, I want to tell you some stuff—you know."

"For *old times* sake." He grins at me.

I know he's mocking me, but I've made up mind to try to do *something*, and I'm determined to see it through. Hope I don't foul-up and bust him a good one before I finish. "Jonathan, I've got some stuff I've wanted to say for a long time." We're sitting on the grass now, not looking at each other but sort of looking off at the back of the library. Idlly I notice the windows at the top of the library will prevent anyone from seeing our fight. "Jonathan, I want to talk to you." I begin. "I've got some things I've been wanting to tell you."

"I'm touched, Bub." Jonathan is chewing on a dried crabgrass twig. Now he crosses his arms and leans back against his tree like a cool Dude, a little bored with sentimental fool like me.

I make a humongous effort not to bristle up. It's hard to keep my cool when I've got myself in a beholden spot like this. I try again. "Please Jonathan, just this once. Listen, okay?"

He opens his eyes wide like he's amazed and can't wait to hear my little tale. I just start talking, surprised that I'm actually being cool. Maybe that's because it's the right thing to do.

I tell Jonathan about Auntie and how much she means to me. "Remember how we used to have lemonade and pizza on the back patio, after T-ball practice?" I ask.

He nods slightly without looking at me. He keeps staring off over the top of the library.

Maybe, I tell myself doubtfully, he's listening and thinking. I talk about Dad and his jail time.

"Remember when we were little kids, how we used to go to the cycle shop? I ask. "And that time when he put both of us in the rumble seat of that bike he fixed up? And he swung around all those corners. We'd lean sideways every time, and Dad would look at us kind of like he was mad. And he'd say, "You boys are not having fun, are you? And that would make us giggle even more. Do you remember those times, Jonathan?" I'm staring at him now and he looks at me. My mind is full of memories.

Jonathan twists his mouth in acknowledgement, but he just looks right through me.

I turn away and stare at the back of the library again, still determined to see this through. "Dad got a bum rap, Jonathan, with the jail time, I mean. They did wrong to lock him up, for something he didn't even know had happened." I look at Jonathan again. "It was wrong of you to con the guys into making fun of him, too, Jonathan."

He picks up the twig and starts chewing on it again; sort of glances at me before looking across at the library roof. Then he mumbles. "If you say so, Scott."

I decide to ignore this and go on to tell him about Auntie, Mom and I while Dad was in prison. I tell Jonathan about Mom and I going away, leaving Ridge Point. And then how I was feeling about coming back again. "I'd hoped we could be friends, like we were once, Jonathan." I finish.

Jonathan looks at me and makes a kind of "Harumph" comment. Then he sort of unwinds himself by rolling over in the grass and finally standing up. He brushes off a few imaginary grass leaves as he walks over to his bike, pulls it away from the tree and straddles it. "Okay, Scott," he says almost absentmindedly. Then he looks up. "So I'll send you a bill." At my puzzled look he answers. "You know, a consultation fee. If I'm gonna be your therapist, you'll have to pay up." He grins.

That stings me! Then I remember what Brittany called my ability to laugh at myself. I grin back. I'm thinking of giving him a high-five, but he turns his bike around and heads off down the alley without a word.

I stare after him, wondering what happened. Did he understand me and plan to lay off, and quit egging the guys on me?

I wonder what Aunt Em will think about all this? I will never know, will I? I get such a gut-sucking pain when I think it; my eyes water-up and I set my teeth together hard. I turn my bike toward the nursing home.

It's funny. While I'm thinking that giving Jonathan a good sock upside the head would have been more satisfying, I'm not angry, just sick—big-time. Dad's lessons must have *took*, even though I didn't know I'd been listening. I don't even care that I made myself vulnerable and then got gut-punched. I know that I don't have a friend anymore.—probably not even Rudy. In some way that I don't understand, I've lost my frustration. I tried, and *did* put myself out there; stuck my neck out and got it chopped off, or at least my tender feelings. I almost grin at my own silly self. Maybe Jonathan's right and I *do* owe him for the therapy session.

CHAPTER 10

At dusk I ride back home. I cross Main Street and wave to old Bob Michaels. He's out sweeping off the sidewalk in front of his hardware store.

I get an idea and almost fall off my bike. It's about Sista, the old lady at the nursing home with the bird wing hand. She waits to see people in the lobby. Again today she was waiting for me to come out and go back through the lobby. She's always there, waiting for *someone*, but I never see her with a visitor. With that lap blanket across her stooped shoulders and the snowy head and great eyes bugged-out like antenna, she reminds me of a large crab waiting to ambush a prey. It sounds sinister. Yet, I know without any doubt that Sista is waiting to have a few words with me. She wants to talk to me. And I don't know how any of this has much to do with me or anything else that I can think of. But something else strikes me too, just in passing. Sista's blind.

Turning the corner onto my street, I shrug off all this. I get these highly off-the-wall ideas about a lot of things lately. Maybe our science teacher, Mr. Ingstrom's right when he says teenagers go crazy at thirteen. "*Some* of them recover," He adds, with his duck-lips, I'm-still-searching-for-the-answer, grin.

Later I turn in our driveway and almost fall off my bike for the second time. There is the shiny red car, here! I stare at the enemy's vehicle. DAD'S INVITED THE BLONDE WOMAN *here?*

I've built up a head steam of anger by the time I get to the door and begin to open it cautiously. How could he? I ask myself this foolish question for the tenth or twentieth time since I caught Dad with that woman at the shop. "Jerk!" I mutter this to myself and give the door a kick before walking into the hall.

Mom's here! She, Dad and the intruder all look up from some papers spread out on the coffee table. I stare at them for what seems like a long time and then I croak, "So, you're getting a divorce?"

Mom stands up as I walk over to hug her. She gives me a buss on the cheek and tussles my hair. "Missed you son," she says with a smile; then asks. "What did you say?"

"Missed you too, Mom," I say. I frown over her shoulder at the blonde woman and then at Dad who's pulled up his wing chair near the fireplace like he's cold or something.

Dad stands up now and comes over to give me a playful punch on the shoulder. He squeezes Mom to him and buries his face in her hair for a moment. Our eyes meet and he looks at the blonde woman. "Grace," he says. "This is my son, Scott." He grins at me. "Son, this is Mrs. Tueksberry. She's my parole officer."

I heave a sign like I shifted off a heavy burden. I did! "I thought—I thought." The words don't come to me.

Mrs. Teuksberry smiles at me, puzzled.

I swallow and try again. The words tumble out like little pebbles. "I saw you at the shop one day. You and Dad seemed to be so—uh. You seemed to know each other so well. I thought."

"Scott!" Mom squeezes my shoulder and gives my head a knuckle rub.

Mrs. Teuksberry smiles gently. "Scott you're thinking about when I came to your cycle shop the other day. That was to help your Dad check out a fellow he was planning to buy parts from."

She smiles and I realize that she's got a matronly way about her, and she's really got a nice smile.

"We found out the parts have been used but everything was on the up and up. Your Dad was concerned about the seller. But everything's okay." She touches my shoulder and gives me a quick smile. "And I'd best be on my way. Long drive back to Stockton." She reaches out to squeeze Mom's hand. "Glad I got to see you again, Lyd."

After Mrs. Teuksberry leaves, I just stare at Dad and feel a lot like the jerk

I thought *he* was! He grins at me. "Lyd," he looks at Mom. "I could eat you up; I've missed you so much!" Mom flushes a little and beams at him.

"So Scott-" Dad's got his arm across my shoulders now. "How do you feel about spaghetti for supper? It looks like we've got a lot of catching up to do." We three head down the hall to the kitchen where Dad gets out a package of sauce mix, Mom starts the pasta and I do the bread. It's a good feeling to know I'll be able to tell my parents what's been going on.

Mom says confession is food for the soul, and she's probably right. It worked its own kind of special miracle today after I talked with Jonathan.

As we eat our spaghetti I'm thinking that I'm a pretty lucky kid. There are still all the problems I had before. But some things I just can't fix. Maybe I didn't make the team in baseball this year. I mean, for instance, well—maybe baseball is not my life's calling. Maybe I'll make the team of people who help out old and lonely people in the nursing home.

When I think of losing Aunt Em I feel sick at heart. But like the preacher said the other night— "death is not the final stopping place; it's a waiting place. God will call up those that love him to be in heaven." I'm not sure what all that means, but I guess I will know someday. If God took up some dirt or dust off the ground, like the pastor says God did, and then that God squeezed in it the shape of a ma and then breathed on it to make it alive—then it does look like the preacher could be right about dying and all that.

I stop eating and look at Mom. She's always been plain Mom; nothing fancy about her. But she's different from a lot of people. I mean it's like she's a real person, what you might call authentic. I'm not afraid that she'll get all gussied up one day and start looking for another lifestyle. I want to tell her "thanks" for coming back. Now she catches me staring at her and stares back, and I can see a kind of affirming look in her light hazel eyes. It's like she's telling me, "I'm Scott's Mom and Nick Gully's wife. It's my role in life. I'm thoroughly enjoying it right now." I give her a Rudy-type of smile.

"I missed you Mom, and I'm glad you're my Mom," I say this quickly and turn back to my spaghetti. After a moment I look up to see Dad grinning at me.

"So," he says, "no more rock throwing, eh?"
"No sir," I answer. "I'm just going to start taking things as they come."

THE END

Printed in the United States
55137LVS00005B

9 781424 108565